My First

Disney Classics
LIBRARY

A Terrific Tea Party

PaRragon

Bath · New York · Singapore · Hong Kong · Cologne · Delhi
Melbourne · Amsterdam · Johannesburg · Auckland · Shenzhen

This edition published by Parragon in 2010

Parragon
Queen Street House
4 Queen Street
Bath BA1 1HE, UK

Adapted by Annie North Bedford
Illustrated by Disney Storybook Artists
Designed by Jerome Rebeiro

ISBN 978-1-4454-2410-1
Printed in China

A Terrific Tea Party

Annie North Bedford

It was morning on Cherry Tree Lane. Admiral Boom had shot off his morning cannon to give the day a proper start. Miss Lark, in the biggest house on the lane, had sent her dog Andrew out for his stroll.

But in the nursery at Seventeen Cherry Tree Lane, Jane and Michael Banks were still in bed.

'Up, up!' said Mary Poppins, their nanny. She pulled back the children's blankets with a firm, but kind hand. 'We'll have no lounging about on a supercalifragilistic day.'

'Supercali-what, Mary Poppins?' asked Michael.

'Close your mouth, Michael,' said Mary Poppins. 'We are not codfish. Supercalifragilistic, of course. If you can't think of a word that says just what you want to say, try supercalifragilistic. And it just describes today.'

That got Jane and Michael up, dressed, and fed in record time.

'Out to the park we go,' said Mary Poppins, hurrying them into their hats and coats. 'Spit spot, this way.'

'Supercalifragilistic!' sang Jane and Michael as they marched along the lane. They almost bumped into Mary Poppins when she stopped to speak to Andrew, Miss Lark's little dog.

'Slower, please,' said Mary Poppins. 'I can't understand a word you say.'

'Yip yap yap,' said Andrew.

'Again?' said Mary Poppins.

'Yap yap,' said Andrew.

'Yes, of course,' said Mary Poppins. 'I'll go straight away. And thank you very much.'

'Yap,' said Andrew.

Taking Jane and Michael by the hand, Mary Poppins started off walking in the direction from which Andrew had come.

'What did he say?' asked Jane.

'He said, "You're welcome",' said Mary Poppins.

'But what else did he say?' Jane insisted.

'I don't think he said anything at all,' Michael said crossly. 'And I thought we were going for a walk in the park.'

'There's been a change of plans,' said Mary Poppins. 'Come along, please. Don't straggle.'

At a brisk pace, Mary Poppins led Jane and Michael down narrow, twisting streets that they had never seen before. Finally, they reached the door of a small house and stopped.

Rap, rap went the parrot-head handle of Mary Poppins's umbrella. The door was soon answered by Mary's friend Bert.

'How is he?' Mary Poppins asked.

Bert shook his head. 'Never seen him like this,' he answered. 'And that's the truth.'

Bert opened the door wide and Mary Poppins pushed Jane and Michael along, in front of her. They found themselves in a large, cheerful room. In the centre of the room stood a table set for tea.

'Bless—bless my soul,' gurgled a voice that was rich with chuckles. 'Is that Mary Poppins? I'm delighted to see you, my dear.'

Jane and Michael looked about. They could see no-one in the room until Mary Poppins spoke. 'Uncle Albert, you promised not to go floating around again!' she said. She seemed to be speaking to the ceiling.

Jane and Michael looked up. There in the air sat Uncle Albert, chuckling merrily.

'I know, my dear,' said Uncle Albert, wiping a merry eye. 'I tried, really I did. But I do so enjoy laughing, you know.' Each time his chuckles bubbled up, he bobbed against the ceiling. 'And the moment I start—hee hee—it's all up with me.' Then he whispered to the children, 'It's laughing that does it, you know.'

Jane and Michael were trying to be polite. They kept their faces straight, but laughter started to sparkle out of their eyes. Then the laughter bubbled up their throats. And soon, they began to chuckle.

By this time, Bert was rolling about, shaking with laughter. As they watched, he rose into the air and was soon bobbing about beside Uncle Albert.

Michael's chuckle grew to a laugh. So did Jane's. Soon, they were filled with laughter. It bubbled out, and they felt lighter and lighter until their feet left the floor and up they floated. Within moments, their heads bumped the ceiling!

'How nice,' said Uncle Albert. 'I was hoping you'd turn up. Do make yourselves comfortable, my dears.'

'I must say you're a sight, the lot of you,' said Mary Poppins, her arms folded in a way that showed her disapproval.

'You know, speaking of sights,' said Bert, 'that reminds me of my brother who has a nice, cushy job in a watch factory.'

'Is that so?' said Uncle Albert. 'What does he do?'

'You know what he does?' gasped Bert, who was laughing so hard that he could barely speak. 'He stands around in this watch factory all day and makes faces.'

And with that, all four of them roared with laughter so much that they turned somersaults in the air.

'I found a horseshoe today,' said Bert, holding his sides. 'You know what that means?'

'I certainly do,' said Uncle Albert. 'It means that some poor horse is walking around in his stockinged feet.'

Again, the room rocked with laughter. But Mary Poppins looked stern. 'This is the most disgraceful thing I've ever seen,' she snapped, 'or my name isn't Mary Poppins.'

'Speaking of names,' said Bert, 'I know a man with a wooden leg named Smith ...'
'Really?' chortled Uncle Albert. 'What's the name of his other leg?'
More gusts of laughter sounded.
'Now then—Jane, Michael!' Mary Poppins said firmly from below. 'I will not have my schedule disrupted.'

'Oh, please stay!' begged Uncle Albert. He waved at the table on the floor. 'I have a splendid tea waiting for us—if you could, er, manage to get the table to ...'

With a rattle and a bump, the table began to jerk. Then up it rose through the air—cups, biscuits, teapot, and all.

'Oh, splendid! Splendid! Thank you, my dears,' said Uncle Albert. Then he said to Michael and Jane, 'Keep your feet back, my dears. Watch the cups and mind the jam.'

'I suppose you'll be wanting me to pour,' said Mary Poppins with a sigh. And up she floated, neat as you please, without so much as a smile.

The others still laughed and bobbled about as Mary poured and passed the tea. 'Thank you, my dear,' said Uncle Albert. 'I'm having such a good time. I wish you could all stay up here with me always.'

'We'll jolly well have to,' Michael grinned. 'There's no way to get down.'

'Well, to be honest,' said Uncle Albert, 'there is a way. Just think of something sad, and down you go.'

But who could think of anything sad? They chuckled at the very idea.

'Time to go home!' Mary Poppins's crisp and firm voice cut sharply through the laughter.

And suddenly, at that sad thought, down came Jane, Michael, Bert, and Uncle Albert. Bump, bump, bump, bump on the floor.

Mary Poppins led Jane and Michael to the door. Bert went with them, too.
'Goodbye,' said Michael. 'We'll be back soon.'

'Oh dear,' Uncle Albert sobbed as he waved goodbye. 'It makes me so sad to see them leave.'

Back home, Jane and Michael tried to tell their father about their adventure. 'We floated in the air and had tea on the ceiling,' Jane began.

'And there was this man with a wooden leg named Smith,' Michael chimed in.

'Poppins!' cried Mr Banks. 'What is the meaning of this?'

'Children will be children,' said Mary Poppins. 'And these two are up past their bedtime. Spit spot.' And she marched the children off to the nursery.

Michael and Jane just looked at each other. 'Anyway,' Jane said as she kicked off her slipper, 'it was a supercalifragilistic day!'

The End.